Interviewing

The Woman

Called Wife

By: Rose Griffin

I Dedicate This Book To My Son Alex: This book was pushed out in a labor of Love, My son Alex, toiled with me, as I filled my heart with sadness and darkness, He sat with me while I tried to understand my assignment and how I could get to the next level, Although I did not agree with some of his measures, I eventually used them to push me to the next level. It was hard finding the right words, as I set out to uncover the truth. So, I say Thank You Alex.

You are fierce and Powerful, may all your dreams be met with a yes and Amen.

Upton Turrell Publishing

398 24th Avenue # 505

Apalachicola Florida 32320

Uptonturrellpublishing@yahoo.com

ISBN:979-8-9878745-2-3

Copyright: Library of Congress:

101 Independence Ave SE

Washington, DC 20540

Message from the Author

I as a person who has used Pen and Paper to express myself for the better part of my life, has added a new version of an old story. I have spent many years honing my craft, sometimes it does not fit into the ideas of others, but I have long since given up on the idea, that I can please people always, I do hope you enjoy my version of Interviewing the Woman Called Wife.

I am also the Author of: Ready for the Wedding, Not Prepared for the Marriage The Politician and I: Inside the Heart of Kevin Begos, and My Inside Voices

Table of Content

Thank You Alex Pg.2

ISBN Information Pg.3

Words from Author Pg.4

Table of Content Pg.5

Introduction Pg.6

I am Elizabeth / Chapter 1, Pg.12

Sure Am / Chapter 2, Pg.28

That Man Was Crazy / Chapter 3, Pg.51

This is not Funny / Chapter 4, Pg.61

Almost Sold / Chapter 5, Pg. 68

I'm Going Home / Chapter 6, Pg.79

Introduction

On assignment one summer, I headed to the village of Uz, (Job's Town). Upon my arrival it was clear to see that they were preparing for some type of celebration, usually the kind of feast that came after a victorious battle. My assignment was to do an interview with the Woman they called "Wife", apparently, at some point in the battle of wits between God and Satan, she deliberately with malice of forethought, decided to encourage her husband (Job), to Curse God and Die, as the story is told.

The scriptures along with some biblical scholars reference her as a trouble maker, an annoyance or agitator; although no one could truly answer the question, as to why this woman said what she was accused of saying. This was yet to be determined.

As a reporter, I immediately had thoughts, my first thoughts were, who was this woman and how was she so insignificant, that they didn't even care enough to give her a name. Which drew me in even closer, I wondered if she had been nameless at home, I wondered if her children had respected her in her mothership capacity, I wondered if her husband respected her as a wife. something more plausible than just "Curse God and Die"!!!!!! had to be her nameless legacy, I have searched the scriptures and searched them again, just for a simplified answer, there were none. I would like to believe she wasn't a mad woman, an evil person or some satanic being, as is suggested by what is presented. When my attention was first directed to this woman, I felt a sense of pity for her. This woman so insignificant, they did not even think her to be worthy of having a name. To feel so insignificant and yet have given birth to countless children, to have stood by the side of a man who barely recognized her.

As a reporter I struggled with all those questions, why on that specific day did she scream CURSE GOD AND DIE. I would like to believe she wasn't a mad woman, evil person or mean and unfeeling woman. I knew that perhaps this wasn't the whole story, but it was the one I had been commissioned to tell. So, what was it about her, that made her not even worthy of a name? Questions filled my mind, how can we say for certain she wasn't used to produce kids and then discarded, as some used up rag? How do we know she wasn't a slave, how can we say for certain, she hadn't been a 13-year-old, who by fate was given over into marriage to some old man, for his bountiful gifts to her family? Who is to know? How and why did this woman scream Die. I then suggest as a reporter, that I examine the testimony of words.

Before writing this story, I decided to seek out some people who may have known this woman for years; this would allow me to paint an accurate portrait of her. I began

my quest at a well, on the south side of Job

Ville, while walking by this well, I heard a

grumpy voice say; aren't you the lady whom

has come to see the woman called Wife?

Chapter 1

I am Elisabeth

I said yes, I am, she then said, I am Elisabeth and wife is my friend. We shared most of our lives in the fields working wheat, and then she scoffed and said; "until Job married her and removed her from her Castle". Then Elisabeth offered me a drink from her well and we sat down to talk. Elisabeth looked me square in the face and said, "they lied"! I said who lied; she said everyone. So, I sat there hoping she would clarify.

She said wife wasn't always mean, her smile lit up the sky brighter than the diamond in our mines, her laughter could be heard for miles and she walked with a sway that said she knew she was special, and that god had blessed her. But in the span of one day, all her dreams vanished right before her eyes and she vanished along with them. Elisabeth went on to say that; Wife was soft and loved to hug, she kissed cheeks in the market, she fed the hungry, she volunteered at the orphanage, and she gave money to the poor. Elisabeth called her an honor to follow; she made reference to the fact that wife, had dreams that were higher than the mountain, including the fact that wife had a way with numbers, she was money smart, she left her castle and instantly began to manage Jobs house as if she was born to do so.

Elisabeth said it had been more than 20 years since she had sat with wife or had shared more than a passing glance, because once she married Job, she lost her right to socialize with the working class. So, a simple hello and a sideways wink every now and again, was the extent of our intertwining, I would smile secretly, and I always kept my head down, as I passed her. Inwardly I would gleam, just from knowing my feisty friend still lived. (She hung her head and began to draw circles in the dirt), as she recounted the day she had heard about wife losing all her children, I could tell by Elisabeth's crumpled shoulders that this memory caused her pain, she repeated the phrase continually "in a matter of minutes they were all gone". All of them, gone, they simply vanished. She quickly leaned into me and whispered, I won't even begin to mention or discuss the talk around town about Job, being on a death bed of affliction. Then Elisabeth sighed shook her head and said, I wondered how much more my poor friend would be able to take.

Long before any of this happened, I can recall all the people who sat at the gate, along with the elders and Job. How they would make mention, of the fact, that job looked as if he was already dead. A couple of them said his children would fetch a pretty penny once he was dead, seeing that they were well groomed and educated. I even allowed myself to wonder how desperate wife could have been, when thinking, that soon her sons would or could be sold as labored workers and her daughters pawned off or forced to marry some leachy handed, old enough to be their grandfather man. After hearing some of the things I had heard, I abandoned my usual pathway home; I started walking the long path just in case my old friend needed me, a shoulder to cry on or a friend to share secrets with, as we had done, in the golden days.

I glanced over at Elisabeth, just in time to catch the lines of tears as they flowed down her cheeks, I felt a sharp sadness in my chest, as the foggy glaze covered her doe shaped brown eyes. I sat there silently wondering, what she would reveal next, what memory would she or could she share. She cleared her throat and began to trace the ground again. As if she snapped out of a trance, she said did you know wife sang? Ohhhhh yes, she sang songs that could put the angels to shame, smiling, Elisabeth cupped her hands leaned back, closed her eyes and said, she sang in the morning, noon time and at night, she sang for her children, she sang for her husband, she sang for her god, oh yeah, she knew god, she loved him, she honored him and she believed in him.

She began to whisper again, by this time I had adjusted my ears to her whispers, (in my mind) I knew what she was about to say, would be great). As she leaned in to me, she said, now what I'm about to tell you need not be mentioned again, (she paused waiting for me to confirm,, that I would not pass this information on). I nodded quickly; because I did not want to miss, what I thought could be a very exciting part of this conversation.

She said, the circle of city folks said, the stench of Jobs sores, could be smelled from one end of the street to the other, and they wondered how wife, bathed him, washed his clothing, fed his kids, always kept their house clean and still showed herself to be presentable in public? They wondered why she did not smell, they wondered if she had contracted the deadly disease Job had.

Some even guessed that perhaps the kids would get it next. In fact, there were those who would walk away, each time she entered the market. There were those whose children were not allowed to play with wife's children anymore. There were those who at one point would sit in the cool of the day and share lemonade with wife, but not now, all her uppity friends had vanished, they would cross to the other side of the street, every time she walked near them. "Poor Wife" Elisabeth said; as she wiped her tears with the end of her hand made lilac apron. Wife's life had taken a tragic turn, but every time you saw wife, she smiled as if nothing in her life had changed. She was beautiful inside as well as outward, to be honest, I knew she was drifting away, although she smiled, but as her true god given friend, I longed for the cheeky girl who had luster in her voice and cheer in her heart. But of lately, there was only silent false greetings, the kind that satisfied the public and would keep the gossip down to a minimal.

The children were sad, oftentimes they did not understand, why their friend could not come over and play, they did not understand, why going to the middle of the town and splash under the water fountain was forbidden, they wondered why there were no more sleepovers. And as always, Wife was left with the task of explaining to her children, why they no longer could enter the school, they would have to sit on their veranda as their mother taught them lessons, these lessons were not only about ABC's, they were also about why they now felt abandoned. Usually wife would begin her stories with you all know god loves us, but as time passed, months and months drug on. She with less and less enthusiasm relied on those phrases as much. She had decided not to say it any more, she reasoned with herself that it wasn't that she didn't believe, she just felt that until something changed, she could see no reason to fill her kids head with things, she wasn't really sure about herself.

I will never forget the sound of the evening bell as it rang time and time again, which was the sound used to symbolize death, the bells tolled when someone's life had ended, and it rang loudly for about 5 hours. I began to look outside but I saw nothing, not that I would have, wife lived in a Huge Mansion on the other side of town, near the wells.

But I would have never guessed, she would fall victim to the wiles of good and evil.

I looked up and within what seemed like minutes darkness had begun to set in, I hadn't noticed how the time had flown, so I said well Elisabeth, thank you for your time but I must be getting along now, Elizabeth smiled and said glad I could help. I said; thank you and maybe we can sit again before I leave town. At this time, I was about six people behind on my list and I had only questioned one, I did not intent to spend so much time in one place. So, I shook the dirt from my behind and began walking.

Wow, I spent all day with Elisabeth and she wasn't even one of my listed people. Wishing I could question more people tonight, I hadn't planned on spending no more than perhaps two or three days on this journey, it is much too late to go to my next person's house; I will rejoin my quest in the morning, I was so very excited, if tomorrow turned out as well as today, I would be on my way really soon, I washed up, climbed into my soft quilted bed and fell fast asleep.

I am so hungry is all I could say, I got

dressed and hurried across the street to the

diner, maybe if I filled myself with pancakes

I could make it until late afternoon. As I

opened the diner's door, a young voice said;

so you're the nosey lady asking questions

about wife?

Chapter 2

Sure Am

I quickly turned to see who had spoken and about to get on my last nerves, (I took a deep breath thinking, it's too early for this). It just so happened to be a boy, sitting there with no legs, right at the diner's door, I said excuse me are you talking to me, He said "Sure Am", are you her or not? I then, with a tone of (how dare you) said well if your referring to MY JOB as a RE-POR-TERRRRR, trying to explain my authority

and right to be here. He then looked at me
and said well come on, I guess I have time
to talk.

I was thinking, who said I wanted to talk
to you. He then looked at me and said, well
what you waiting on? you gotta push my
chair, can't you see I do not have legs? I
really want to slap him or maybe I just
wanted to laugh, this kid was rude and
funny. Ok, so I pushed him, (what was I to
do) while he instructed me on where to go,
where to turn and why I was rudely hitting
bumps, which I might add was a dusty

bumpy rock road. We ended up in front of a persimmon tree, huge tree with what seemed to be hundreds of persimmons, dripping with juice, plump and ready for the picking. No sooner had I wanted to grab one and bite into it, he said this is my tree and yes you can have some, I'm sure you're hungry, I noticed you haven't eaten today, I was then again thinking that's because you stopped me from eating Mr. Nosey Big Mouthed Boy.

But being that I hadn't eaten since earlier the day before, I hurriedly pulled one from the tree. Oh my god!!!! It tasted so sweet, I buried my face deep inside it, the juice surrounded my mouth and my stomach screamed with delight as, the juice slid down my throat. He grinned happily and said you love it don't you, I said yes, he then went on to explain that this tree was his life, his future and the only reason he was alive and able to take care of himself. He said as a child he lost his legs and his parent could not care for a cripple child, they had no other choice but to place him in an orphanage. They were poor farm working people, whom already had four other children to look after, being crippled, makes it difficult to find a suitable person to watch him daily, because both his parents needed to work. So off to the orphanage he was sent, not because they didn't love him, they had no other choice and besides, there was someone always there to look after his needs. Well the physical ones anyway he said as he shrugged his shoulder.

He slowly looked up at me with a small crackling tone, and said Ma'am have you ever had a belly full of food, but your heart still felt empty? I surely did miss my momma and my sisters, I cried myself to sleep every day for four years, until that day.

I wanted to say what day? But this child was

strange, so I just waited on the answer or

him to stop talking. He looked up again at

me, that is when I saw the hugest grin, I had

ever seen in my life. I could not take the

suspense any longer, I screamed "boy spill

it"!!!!!, He laughed so loud his whole body

shook, I just knew he was going to fall out

of that chair. Finally, he said, yepppp, I

knew you were nosey. I wanted to knock

him out, but instead I began to laugh, after

about ten minutes of me laughing, we finally

settled down and this serious calm look entered his eye.

That's when he said she saved me, she loved me, and she made sure I was never empty again. She!!!!! Who??? Is what I said? He looked at me angrily; face frowned from top to bottom. Didn't you say you came here to talk about wife? Well why do you think I brought you here, this is my story about wife. A look of amazement touched my heart as I sat down, now with another persimmon in my hand; I said I'm sorry begin please. He said on the day he became twelve, it was a custom of his

people that a young boy becomes a man. So,

on that day he was ejected from the

orphanage, with two sandwiches and five

dollars, which was a lot of money in those

days, but because he had never dealt with

money, within minutes he had fallen victim

to a scam, and lost all his money, too two

crafty boys sitting by this very same tree.

They offered themselves as helpers,

ready to push him around in his chair, if he

would pay, he then told them he only had

five dollars; they also said, he could live

with them under the same five-dollar deal. Thinking this must be his lucky day, he gave them the money, but instead of helping they laughed, called him gullible and ran off. He chuckled and said, "what was I going to do run after them". And looked at his bottom area, where what use to be his legs lived. I understood exactly what he was thinking, I myself had dealt with issues, love, trust and the lack there of, I kind of liked being a reporter, it kept me on the go, I did not have to stay in any one place too long, and I did not have to become familiar with any one set of people. This was very good for me because I did not trust anyone, at any time, for any reason. My life's experiences taught me to never, never and I mean never, let anyone into my heart again.

Although I hadn't heard his story yet, but from where I stood, I could just imagine his tale would be hard, as I imagined everyone's were, because mine had been. I guess I should not project my hardships, disbelief and total lack of love, trust or understanding for people onto my subjects. But as I had done this for years, I could always draw empathy for those I interviewed, but never did I get to the place of sympathy because my mind would always analyze them, while dissecting their stories.

Although it was plain to see most of them spoke their truths, but inside my broken vessel, I had no way of releasing my pain, therefore I could not see or feel theirs. Such a disaster when you are the reporter assigned to report the truth. You sometimes confuse the truth with your truth and if you are not careful you can get lost in your stories. That has truly happened to me a couple of times, so I try my very best to shake the dust and former things, of my life,

off my feet, before I set sights on any single

person.

    He then went on to tell me the story of

Wife, he said after two days and nights of

sitting there alone, hungry, crying, lost,

confused, wet from urine and feces,

(apparently the ladies of the orphanage did

all his cleaning, bathing of him, sitting him

on the pot and cleaning his rear end. He had

never learned how to perform that task),

being on his own now; he wasn't even able

to help his self from his chair. During his

sleeping last night, he somehow fell from his chair. He laughed and said; "I woke up face first in these persimmon's, I hadn't eaten in two days, so I grabbed one and began eating, smelling like a stuck pig, left out in the sun, what was I going to do, flies swarmed around me and the sun baked all the filth to my skin, but I could not move or I did not know that I could move, let's just say that."

That's when I heard that voice, apparently, she thought I was dead, she said poor poor young man, is he dead, is he alive? I was too afraid to open my eyes, so I just laid there. One voice sounded really old said no ma'am he isn't dead, but he surely does smell like he's dead. She said well put him up on the wagon and bring that chair also. I felt something soft and prickly touch my back and face, she said I wonder who he belongs too, why haven't anyone noticed him missing, he smells as if he been gone for weeks and without any water on his body, clean clothing or food. I bet his mother is worried sick and do you see, his legs are missing as well. Well I can't imagine what fear is racing through the people who are looking for this child.

41

After riding for a while, she said put him in that tub of water and do not let him drown. He's probably too weak to hold himself up, well, that wasn't a lie, the cold water gave me no other choice but to open my eyes and scream. She laughed and said I knew you were ok, I saw your eyes moving the entire drive back, now do you have a name Mr. Coma Patient, he then smiled and said; she was really funny, and she was really pretty. He shifted several times in his chair, as if he was positioning himself to say something uncomfortable, tears began to roll down his young face, his cheeks became hot and red, as if they were on fire. He looked up at me and said, without a second thought she loved me, with all of her heart, she loved me instantly, as if I was one of her own.

I'm not of any type lineage or blood relations to her, so it took a minute for the family to warm up to me, but eventually they did. I wasn't allowed to sleep inside the home, but I had a cottage, a bed, a toilet, a towel of my own, and a set of soft sheets. None of those things mattered as much, as did my nightly routine of myrrh and spice oils, she had her maids to rub down my skin, she said it would eventually help my skin return to life, "and dog gone it"!!!! After a few weeks I felt softness like them prissy girls did. (He looked at me and grinned) as if the world was alright with him. He said do you have prissy girl skin, he kind of caught me off guard, the only comeback was the truth and I told him no one had ever asked me that before, but I'm sure I did not have any prissy girl skin, I then thought, "I surely hope not", I pride myself on being self-sufficient and prissy girl skin would be a setback.

Myrrh was one of the things they produced at wife's home, not inside her home but in one of the barns out on the range, much farther out than my cottage. Boats would bring in the shrubbery from the near east, this shrubbery and trees were mashed, grounded and processed into oils, which were then in turn, sold for a magnificent price, it was usually sold to royals and people who could easily afford it. That is where wife came in; she was good at adding other ingredients and spices to bring the oils to their full potential. She was a wizard at selling, buying and producing money, as if she was born for that job. I often would hear the grinders say, because of wife's imagination and giving heart they flourished, they were allowed to take samples of the finished product home for themselves or as treats for their family members. Most of her workers could not normally afford the price of those oils.

But nevertheless, they all wore the scents of royalty, which was said to bring all the workers joy both male and female. I asked the young man; well if you're so close to her, why did she allow you to be in that diner away from home, alone and with no travel companions to push you? He scoffed, as if I was on the wrong boat, then he said; just let me tell my story, you're so nosey. Apparently after about a year of doing the minor chores, learning to get around on some walking stick that she commissioned, learning to bath, I became good at getting in and out of bed, and getting dressed. I became so good at it, I learned to wash my own clothing, in a hot pot out back of my cottage, I became almost independent and as the grinders referred to me as the "kid with the nose", I learned that I knew the difference in the oils just by smell and I became the smeller, not just any smeller, but the smeller for wife's products. So are you saying, when you asked me to push you, you were able to do it yourself. With a wide-open grin, he said; Yes ma'am, I surely can, but then I started thinking, she's nosey and wants information, I may as well make her work for it.

Well, all I could do was laugh and shake my head, I had been gotten by another man, but this one had baby prissy girl skin and no legs. How dare I fall for the "oh poor pitiful me" game once again. He finally took in a deep breath and said well It's getting late, I have work to do, I can't be wasting all my day chitter chatting with you. Don't you have some reeee portttttt inggggggg to do? He then turned his wheel chair around and rode off, reminding me not to take too many of his persimmons.

Here I go again, I spent all days with another person who wasn't even on my list, I gotta stop doing this, I need to get on track, if I am to get the story of wife and get it from accurate, credible sources, those kinds who can add a little flare to my piece. I guess I better head back to town, grab me something to eat, get a good night's sleep and try it again tomorrow. Lordy, Lordy its morning already, I hear the gentleman I am to interview, lives only three blocks from where wife's children were, when they all died. This should make for a fascinating story, I can't wait to hear his side of this tragedy.

Chapter 3

That Man was Crazy

Good morning is Thomas here, I am the reporter, whom he spoke with regarding information related to the woman called wife. "Good morning", was the gentle voice which came from the inside of a slightly cracked door. Thomas is my husband, but he isn't here at the moment, may I help you? Well ma'am, I was to interview him, he had agreed to give me specifics on wife, her life, her time and her tragic story. I have been meaning to speak with him for the pass two days, but other things hindered me, do you know when he will return? no I do not, but I'm sure my words are just as important as his.

She opened the door, I almost gasped for breath I thought, "oh my what a beautiful woman, her skin had a dark tint almost regal, and her hair was a mixture of dark black and shiny gray", never have I witnessed a glow as the one of this woman, I stared at her intently, she asked sharply, is something wrong, I said no; she then said well, why are you searching my countenance from head to toe, I plainly

stated that her beauty was bold. She smiled

and said I gather you haven't seen wife,

because my looks pale in comparison to

hers. She told me to have a seat, with two

small cups and a large pitcher of something,

she sat in front of me, she then said well

what do you want to know.

I struck out running, I was on a time

schedule and I had no more time to waste, I

said; what is the real story on her, was she

sweet, kind and humble or was she the mean

unforgiving person, who hated god and

wanted her husband to die? The woman took a deep breath and said "He was crazy", I said who was crazy, she said lets not beat around the bush, you know who I mean, who else would sit around and live in agony for that man years, who else would allow someone as sweet as wife to suffer the way she did, who in their right frame of mind, would not cover themselves in sackcloth and ashes, long enough to repent for their sins, so that his family would not pay the price, for his sin.

She poured both her and I a cup of a fruity smelling yellowish orange mixture, she also placed a bowl of warm cinnamon bread on the table, she said, drink and eat, this is going to take some time. She dipped her bread in the juice, took a bite and said, the juice you are drinking and the bread you are eating are from a recipe wife gave me, when I was newly married. I grabbed the cup and drank hurriedly as if drinking the juice would give me a connection to wife. I assumed the bread to be just as meaningful as the juice, so I bit into the bread as if I was trying to find treasured gold.

She said wife was beautiful, she smelled of exotic scents every day, she never left her home without covering her head as it showed her symbolic respect for her husband, children and family. This beautiful woman's eyes became sullen as she mentioned the love and luster, wife brought to her family and friend, this, woman even made mention of wife as a crusader for the lost and lonely, she said wife was the person you could count on when life got hard, death drew near or some widowed woman, lost all she possessed, and stood to lose even more, wife would stand in the gap for her.

As tears streamed from this woman's eyes, she told me the story of how as a child her parents died, leaving her three sisters and herself to fend for themselves, although they were not poor and did not have to worry about being forced to marry or being sold to the nearest elderly man as a concubine, they were fortunate enough, that her older sister was an astute business woman and did her best to carry them forward for a number of years. She spoke of being the baby of the family and how, she would cry herself to sleep nightly, praying for her mother and father to return. Then she said sadly, in a very low soft voice, but they never came back, so I do understand, the tragic drama wife must be feeling at this season of her life. There were times I would lay in bed shaking from loneliness of not seeing my parents and my eldest sister would not sleep all night, she would lay there with me in her arms, rocking me and singing me songs all night long, she taught me how to be a lady, she educated me, she made sure life was as pleasant for me as possible, there were times when suiters would show up to marry my sister, but she refused to marry because she did not want to leave myself and my other two sisters alone. She sacrificed so much to hold our family together. I then interrupted her chatter, with a question, I do understand you feeling sorry for wife, but why are you recounting the story of your life, when I need help with the story of wife? The beautiful lady smiled at me as she poured me more juice and said because the eldest of my sisters was wife. Therefore, there is nothing Thomas can tell you about wife, that I haven't told him, I spent my life loving wife, as she spent her life loving and raising me as her child, who better to tell you about her than me. She was my sister before she was a wife, mother, queen or even before she helped orphans, fed the poor, made perfumes, owned businesses, she was my sister. I thought, I guess she told me.

I then said well thank you so much, she said she needed to prepare lunch for her husband, I took that as a sign to leave. So I bided her farewell and walked away feeling insightful and educated.

Chapter 4

This is not Funny

I cannot believe I wasted another day, and still I have not spoken to anyone from my list, how can this be, this is not funny. I need to speak to someone from my list, I wonder why Thomas did not stay home long enough for me to get his story? Well, I guess I will walk down on the shore side, to see if I can meet Joseph, someone made mention that he spends most of his days on those shores, fishing and making baskets for the fishermen to carry their fish in. Perhaps if I catch him at the right time, he will help me complete my story, I surely would like to hear someone who truly can open up my eyes to the story of wife, I have this feeling there was more to this woman than meets the eye, I'm sure this lady had depth and tenacity no one could measure, but I surely would love to try, I surely would love to be the one who told her story.

As a person myself, who has had to battle falsehood and misconceptions in my own life, I would love to unearth the story behind the story, because I have had to ride the lightning bolt of people's perceptions, I understand fully how just one false word, could send your life into a spiraling downward stroll, with no end in sight. And regardless to how hard you try there is no fixing, there is not enough praying sometimes, that can change people thoughts of you, even when you are truly innocent, you find yourself battling lies, Those are the times you just wanna crawl under a rock and die, trying to scream to the top of your lungs, for just one person to see the truth and not cater to those horrible lies, that sound good to the tickling of the ear.

So, no this is not funny, I need this story, I am trying to crawl my way out of the darkness, into the marvelous light, I need this chance to reintroduce myself, the pass three years have been hard for me, after a failed marriage, three miscarriages, too much to drink and a host of lying suiters. I just want to refocus my life and establish a new and more improved version of the same old girl. There are no excuses, there are no, one single person I will blame, there are no, because I wasn't loved as a child, there are no, I didn't get enough love or food, there are no, they did not choose me for the team.

Those are not the reasons for my plight, it is just my season for trials and tribulations, it was my season to be sifted as wheat, just incase my usefulness would be called upon, to do a mighty work, it would then be discovered as a qualification. Well, I did not always win, I fell short on some of those occasions, but what I did not do was lay there, I think that's what I'm beginning to think I find fascinating about wife, the more I hear, the more I look into her life, I think I need to discover how she continued to keep going in the presence of all her pain. So, no it's not funny, my life is also depending on the knowledge wife holds. I surely do hope I find the answers for my soul and for the piece I need to complete, in order to prove that I am back in the game, I at one time was a world famous journalist, with more than 200 pieces under my belt, then life threw me to the wolves, and instead of fighting hard to stay on top, I caved in and allowed life's pain to almost take me out, but I'm back and I intend to win this round. Well, that's enough of me feeling sorry for me, I have a job to do, so I guess I will keep walking until I reach the shoreline, I am sure this man called Joseph will have something intriguing to add to the story of wife, his name sounds like he just may be related to someone, who knows something or someone who has mentioned something. I was told he was a very large man, with a very large personality. I was told that if Joseph did not know anything no one would, ok Joseph come on guy make my day.

Chapter 5

Almost Sold

Excuse me young lady, do you know a very large man called Joseph? She frowned, as if I had asked her a very stupid question, I understood the crinkle in her face, as I had used that very same look on countless occasion after being asked question, where I thought should be a crime, to ask such a dumb question. She then said of course I know him, why do you ask and who are you and what is it that you want from him? I haven't seen you around these parts before, are you one of those people sent to

dismantle our belief in Christ, cause if you

are, you are barking up the wrong tree, he's

going to chew you up and spit you out.

Don't say I did not warn you, he won't

take kindly to you, you do not look like us,

you look sort of suspicious if you ask me.

But its not my place to judge, I've been in a

few tight spots myself, and if it had not been

for the woman called wife, there is no telling

where I would be today, Do you know the

woman called wife, I said no I do not (I did

not want to say I was a reporter or that I was

on a quest pertaining to the woman called

wife) so I played it off and let her kept

talking' She then said well that says a lot

about you, because everybody from these

parts knows who wife is. There has been a

lot of controversy surrounding her name,

some say she went crazy, some say she

disrespected god, some say she tried to force

god to kill her, some say grief struck her

down, some say she gave up on god, some

say she stop trusting the power of healing.

But I say, if there was any woman on this

earth who understood the power of love and

helping others, it would have been wife. One day I sat out to go to the market for my ailing mother, some men came along and snatched me, they took me to the center of town where, they were about to sell me, then along came wife, I looked into her eyes, she looked into my eyes and my soul screamed silently please save me, and without hesitation, she asked the body snatchers, how much do you want for her, she would make a great concubine for my aging husband.

At first, I thought oh my god, I am going to be no better off, than if they sold me to some old man, as to his wife buying me for her husband. The men sat a price, wife paid it and said come on girl you got a job to do. My stomach flipped as I thought I will live in hell until I die, what about my poor sick mother, who will care for her, who will gleam the fields to get food and money, my poor mother will surely die, as I stood there with all hope lost, wife leaned in and said; it is all well with you, do not be afraid. Stand up straight, do not ever bend over for anyone, be regal, trust in the timing and know that god has a reason and he is a just god. She took me to the edge of town, she wrote a note of servitude, she said never

leave home without this paper, if you are

ever stopped again, you will appear to be in

my employment. And she also gave me a

half sack of money and told me to do right

by myself and if I ever needed work come

see her, she told me where she lived. I told

her about my mother and how I would

forever be in her debt, she not only saved me

from being almost sold, but she saved my

mothers life also.

I stood there in awe, I as a reporter,

began to question the fore knowledge of this

young woman and wife, I said and this lady

did not know you? she had never

encountered you before? had you ever seen

this woman before? she looked at me again

as if I was crazy, she said cant you hear?

didn't I just tell you we were total strangers,

that's what makes this lady so special she

did not care who I was, whether I was rich

or poor and it was easy to tell that she was

rich, her scent and clothing told the story,

whether I was young or old, she only cared

about the cry for help that leaped out of my

soul and she heard my silent pain. That's

who wife is, anyway I don't know why I'm

telling you all this, you don't even know her and you probably have never been in a situation where you were almost sold and someone save your life, you probably have never been on the verge of total collapsing and someone held you up, you probably have never been hungry and someone fed you. So perhaps I'm speaking in vain. But I love wife with everything, you should meet her, she's better than gold.

Well I won't be wasting your time anymore, with my babblings about wife, as a stranger, you will never know the joys of wife, unless you taste them first hand. And besides you came to see Joseph not me, I'm not sure when he will return, but remember what I told you, he doesn't take kindly to strangers, he doesn't like people asking to many questions and please be careful because his temper hasn't been good as of lately, his sister died, and I think he is in mourning. Well good bye and good luck in your talk with Joseph, perhaps if you come back tomorrow he will be here. As she walked off, A harsh reality hit me, apparently, this is not the story for me, I have spent 4 days in this town looking for a solid story on wife and as of yet, I haven't gotten close to any of the people on my list. I guess I need to give up, squash the whole thing. The only thing about that is, I need this story it is my chance to redeem myself before my peers, colleagues and most definitely my family. I am getting tired and I feel like I am missing something, why is it so hard to find those people that promised me and interview, I just knew they would help me, I traveled 16 hours on this journey, trying to reach this place only to go back empty handed, that is so sad… I'm exhausted, mentally and physically,,,,,

Chapter 6

I'm Going Home

I may as well pack my bags, I am going home, I will catch the next flight out of here, at least I tried, no one can say I did not try. This has been very humbling, I spoke with strangers, I ate dirty fruit, I hardly got a decent meal at a restaurant, I went through the town searching for people who swore they would stand firm for an interview. I had to deal with a sassy persimmon eating kid, and an almost sex trafficked young lady, a sister who would never admit it, even if her eldest sister was wrong, a best friend at a

well and now to have to return home in

shame, unable to pull this story together, all

the interview characters are non-existent.

What a final joke.

I would have loved to had tasted some of

the food from this town, I am sure there

were a lot I missed, maybe I will return one

day, just to sit under the persimmon tree and

find out from that young boy what were the

names of wife's perfumes or what would be

other uses for her spices, were they good for

headaches, could you rub some on your back

just to take away the aches. Or were they good in bath water, would I actually smell like a prissy girl, If I chose to wear them daily, would I find luster if I used them in my hair, would I regain my sense of womanhood and desire to be loved, if I moisturized my body daily? Those are the questions I would ask the Boy.

I then would want to know if Thomas was picked by wife to be Emilia's husband? (Emilia is wife's sisters name). I would have asked Emilia if her sisters sacrifice for all those years, encouraged her to be more like her sister, in loyalty and placing others first and did she stand by her Thomas as wife did Job? Furthermore, I would ask the young girl, if she ever went to work for wife from time to time and did her mother recover from her illness? But my most needed conversation would have come from her friend, the one who loved her and respected her, to the place in her heart, where she would bow her head as she passed wife, as to not disturb her status in society, although they grew up together and they shared many moments, times and secrets we could not ever imagine, she still allowed her best friend to live in her status and she held no ill feeling toward her, she took it upon herself to walk near wife's house regularly, she said just in case wife needed a shoulder to cry on.. I would ask her where can I find a friend like that?

Anyway, my plane will be arriving soon, so I better use the bathroom, I hate bathrooms on planes, they are so uncomfortable, so small and cramped, I always feel as if I may fall in. Excuse me ma'am, (wow!!!! these ladies are so beautiful in this part of the world, she almost reminds me of Emilia, the skin, the hair and the look). Ma'am do you mind if I leave my bag near you? I need to use the restroom and don't want to carry it with me. The lady smiled and said of course you can.

I kindly answered with; Thank you ma'am,

She looked me straight in the eyes, winked and said you are welcome young lady, did you have a wonderful time visiting here, she smiled and said; I said visiting, because you do not look like you are from these parts of the world. I turned just in time to see the (piercing look of a magnificent creature, this woman looked like she belongs near the angels), I smiled and said, thank you for asking, I did not actually come here on vacation, I actually came here as a reporter to interview several people, whom I was told, has knowledge of a woman called wife, they were suppose to had given me the true story of that woman and I in turn would use that story to reclaim my place in the Journalistic World. Well that never happened, I talked to several people who added stories about wife's life, but not one of the ones, whom had given me their word,

84

that they would spare time for me to interview, or shall I say those whom I had made plans on talking too.

The lady smiled and said you sound very disappointed, I do hate your trip did not prosper or gain you the second chance you wanted, perhaps all isn't lost. What questions would you have broached? if you had the opportunity to meet those people from your list? You can use me as a practice person, lets try to find some answers. The fact that this total stranger sat there and was willing to help me warmed my heart. It had been a long time since someone sat there just to listen to me or help me. I thought, she's was very kind, and I appreciated the fact that she would help me for no reason, I could not help myself from staring, she was so pretty and so kind to give of her time in that manner. I said ok, let's do it. After about 30 minutes into us doing the back and forth, while smiling, laughing and coming up with tons of scenarios, she said what about if I pretend as though I was Wife and you asked me questions and I answer them as I feel that she would, does that sound like something we can do? I became excited and said yes, yes, I sounds great.

I squared my shoulders back, then I looked her straight in the eyes and said; hello I am a reporter from Butterfly & Bee Consulting, Marketing and Media Group, I am here on behalf of the media department, I've been assigned the task of interviewing you and am commissioned to produce a piece on you Ma'am, It is so very great to meet you, the first question out of my mouth was, can i begin with why there is no name listed for you except wife? She sat up straight and her voice seemed to grow stronger, (as if that was a touchy subject) I do have a name, my name is Sitidos (Sitis for short) I am also known as Uzit, which is my original name, it is Greek and I am said to be an Arabian Princess.

I bloomed in glee, because somewhere inside of me thought, oh this lady will help me make this story seem real, and I reasoned with myself saying, well at least someone will believe it, although I was thinking all this is going to be a lie, but who will know, I silently thought.

She then said, I hate it when people assume I was some cast away, that my husband picked me up and turned me into the lady of the manor, As it should be known, I was the lady of my own castle before I met him, life hasn't always listed me as the wife of Job, I was once a princess, who was sought after by a great leader, a daring man of god, a man who feared and loved god by the name of Job. I too feared and loved god. Although I am listed as the person who wanted my husband to die, I am also listed as the person who had no respect for god, I am also listed as a crazy woman, not to mention the stories that people tell, whom have no idea about who I am.

First of all, mine and Jobs story has more to it than just 42 chapters, my story reaches from the depth of my soul, to the eternal hell I suffered for over 4 decades, when someone reads about me, they think well her kids died, she lost it all, her husband got sick and she impatiently ordered him to curse god and die, but that is so very far from the truth, someone failed to mention that for over 40 years my husband remained sick, I then went from Princess to common worker, I cleaned out toilets, where I once had folks to clean out mine, I scrubbed floors, where I once had someone to scrub mine, I washed folks clothing, where I once had folks washing mine, for over 40 years my husband stayed afflicted, he wasn't able to provide for us, so I did, I went to work every day, to feed us, to buy us food and him medicine.

And this was after I discovered all of my children dead under a pile of rubble, I ran to the house, I screamed out their names, but none of them responded to my cries, pleas or begs to god. The cattle was gone, the sheep was gone, the horses was gone, the servants were gone, everything creeping or crawling was gone, even the livelihood of my husband was gone, all our friends were gone, except for all the Nay Sayers who sat at the gate, wondering what had we done, to bring this upon ourselves, all the ladies from the social clubs, church groups, prayer groups, all the folks we had loaned money, those ones we had fed when they were hungry, paid bills for and given council to were gone, they no longer wanted to be near me, they assumed my husband had a disease and they would catch it, because I had to have caught it, seeing that I was his wife right. They would cross to the other sides of the road, just so they did not have to say good morning, I had no time to wear fancy clothing or sometimes even brush my hair, I had a charge to keep, everything was gone but him and he was destitute and at deaths door.

For over forty years, as Satan beat on Job, I was beaten too, when he cried out in pain from his sickness, I cried out in pain, because he was my husband and I loved him, when he smelled bad, I smelled bad, it was me who continued to sleep with him, he needed me close, just in case he needed help to the bathroom, or a drink of water, or to give him his doses of medicine. It was me who stood up for him, when folks would say "Job must have sinned mighty bad", I defended his honor. When Satan set out to destroy Job as he was allowed to do, when god told him he could do it, no one considered, that those were my kids too, that was my home too, those were my friend too, those were my cattle too, that was my stable too, that were my scented oil company too. That was my church also, those were my clean clothing and that was my heart and soul being broken too.

I missed my children most of all, they had already suffered long before their deaths to be honest, when their father first became sick and the object of Satan and Gods tug of war. But things became more intense as Job stood firm and Satan became more angry, and God became more determined that Job would prevail, no one ever looked over in the corner, where I spent the next 4 decades crouched in fear, grief and sadness, no one looked over in the corner, where I would cry, as I stood in front of the piled up rubble of a house, where my children corpses lay underneath for decades. No one saw me, as I prayed for years, that maybe just one of them got out and had amnesia from the bricks that hit their heads, but would finally remember me and come home, no one saw me, bent over in agony as I grew weaker daily.

No one saw me as I psychologically diminish, no one ever asked me if I was ok, no one ever sat with me and let me grieve, no one ever bothered to help me bury my children, for over 40 years their bodies stayed buried under a pile of debris and I was forced to look at it daily as I walking from the well to get water, I would pass by my children, I would sit in front of the exploded house and eat my food, the stench for months overwhelmed me, but I sat there anyway, I would leave bread and drink, hoping that if my children's spirits ever became hungry they would eat what I left for them, but when I would return the next day, the food would still be in the bowls and the flies would have overtaken the juice.

All the memories and agony existed daily, as I took out the pot he used, I saw my children, as I sat at night outside trying to find a breath of fresh air, away from the stench of Jobs body, I saw them, I would look over and see the piles that suffocated my babies. I know they called for me, as the fear and smothering of death encamped around them, I know they begged for life, because I had always taught them to pray. I know they needed me, and I was not there, I spent decades feeling like a failure, I could not help my babies live, I was not the author or finisher of protecting them, as I had done throughout the years. I cradled them, breast

fed them, wiped their noses, sang them

songs, read them bedtime stories, cooked

them their favorite meals, helped them with

their school lessons, I had failed my

children, I was thinking, the last thought

they had of me was, where is my momma

and why is she not getting us out?

So, when they say I am mean, when they

say, I told my husband to curse god and die.

when they say, I and standoffish. when they

say, I daydream. Yes I do and did all those

thing, I did not tell him to curse god and die,

because I do not love god, I was so very tired of being hungry, taking care of my husband and he never healing, I was tired of washing out other people pee pots, I was tired of wringing out other people underwear, I was tired of cooking food and not having enough for both of us to eat, I sometimes had only enough to keep him alive, I worked all day and sometime there wasn't enough, my soul needed things I never told anyone about, I needed to bury my children, I wanted them to be in peace, in a clean resting place instead of lying under trash, dust and rocks for 40 years. I wanted to give them a solid place to sleep until the lords return. Those are the things I yearn for, those are the things I cried about, prayed for. Those are the thing that ached inside my heart and cause me a never-ending anger.

I remember coming home one particular night and as I looked at him sitting there, I became mad, mad at God, mad at Job, mad at myself and mostly mad at the lot life had given me, who could have imagined me, a young beautiful Princess, whom had spent the entirety of her life caring for and catering to the needs of others, would now be in a place, where she could not do anything about anything, She prayed, she read her bible, she used all her kindness to draw kindness, she opened up her heart to the needy and the greedy, knowing that God would see me through. So that night, I did not care, I figured if I said the wrong thing to Job, God would cause Job to be taken out of his misery, which in turn would take me out of mine, as if one plus one makes two, if Job dies, so would I.

I thought, if I could get him to cause god to stop the pain, anguish, disgrace, loneliness, shame, confusion and sadness, then I could die, all I wanted was to die and I knew Job was the key to my death. I had lived in this stone-cold hell for decades and regardless to whatever I did or said nothing changed, nothing improved nor would it, I had come to a fork in the road and that road said, useless highway, dead end valley. She then took a deep breath, (oh, what a beautiful lady) I thought as I gazed deeply into her eyes, then then sighed, as if she wanted to burst open, she lowered her head as to gather her composure. After some time, she returned to our conversation, with the clearing of her throat. I immediately said, so wife what happened next? She said there is so much to tell, I don't know where to begin. She smiled and said; I really don't know child, she said do you have children? I shook my head no. She said; I'm sorry for you. I felt a tingle of sadness, I don't know why, perhaps I was thinking, she knew something about motherhood, I would never know.

She said can I share a secret with you, again I shook my head with a firm yes. She said you gotta promise me you will never share this information. I said; no ma'am I won't tell a soul. She then went on to tell me of her anger, her anger with God and how since her parents death she remained steadfast in her love for god and people, how she sacrificed her life to raise her siblings, feed the poor, pray often, employ others so that they in turn could feed their families, she said, I tried to live a solid life, she said, she assumed if she lived right and obeyed the commandments life would go smoothly for her. She said, never in a million years would I have believed, everything I held dear would vanish in one day, she said never in a million years would she ever had believed, that her pain would come from the same place she found so much joyous peace.

She stood up as if she was going to walk off, but instead she kneeled beside me and grabbed my hand, she squeezed it firmly, took another deep breath and said with tears streaming down her round cheeks, "I never asked for much, I never asked for much of anything", I found my life to be full of the things I desired most. Family, Love and Being my Brothers Keeper, those are the things that brought me joy and peace. But I will never forget that day, it was a chilly day, I woke early, I fed my husband, cleaned his wounds, changed the bandages on his wounds, which took two hours because he had so many sores, I remember picking up the pot to go empty it, so that he would have a clean pot to relieve himself, on my way back from the outhouse, I looked over the field where my children still laid in a destitute state.

As if they were cast-away, no burial, no preacher, no words or passage of right, no caskets, no nothing, just still lying under rubble for over 40 years, something struck my soul that morning, I thought the least that could have been done for my precious babies, would have been a decent funeral service. Because, as I stood there I thought, I never got a chance to say good bye, I never got a change, to tell them how they made my life worth living, I will never get the change, to sit my baby girl on my lap and rocked her to sleep ever again, I never got a change to make sure they understood, just how deeply their impact to my heart reached. So, I thought, lets bury them, lets get them in a warm peaceful ground, a resting place at least until god came back for them. I rushed back up to the house where my husband was finishing his breakfast.

As I entered the door I heard voices, those were his two friends who had (despite everything), they still remained by his side, (although they would sometimes make mention of the fact, that they did not understand why god hadn't healed him yet, but other than that, they stayed with him while I worked). I ran up to one of his friends and I said would you please help me dig my children up from under those bricks, so that I can give them a decent burial. He said yes, But, all of a sudden, a thunderous voice came up out of Job and he said no, he would not allow his friend to help, he said that the children were not under there and that they were already gone with God.

I turned around and stared him in his eyes, I wanted to say you must be a mad man, how dare you say they are not there, when I sat there for months breathing in the odor of decay, death, agony, defeat and sheer grief as it poisoned my very core, I wanted to say where were you when I heard the voices of my children cry out to me day and night, as I sat there, winter, spring, summer and fall, year after year, where were you? when I placed food there just in case they became hungry, where were you? when I lost weight, lost my hair, lost my dreams, hopes and desires.

I did not utter a word, I hung my head and I walked off, because although I wanted to scream, throw something, cry, call him a liar, even pour the pee pot on his head, I did nothing, because he was still my husband and I still loved and respected him, I would have never brought shame to my family or the memory of my children nor their father. So, I said nothing. I slowly walked out the door, I headed straight way to the pile of rubble, I stopped along the open field and I picked some purple flowers, the kind I use to use when I made the oils, I placed them ever so carefully on the rubble and I told my children good bye, I kissed the ground and I kissed some rocks, I called out each of my children names and I told them how sorry I was, for not being able to save their lives, I told them how sorry I was, for not being able to wash their hair, kiss their wounds, and listen to their stories of school lessons, I told them how much I missed them, I told them how much I craved their love and the sparkle in their eyes, I told them that each of them held a gigantic place in my heart, each one separate, but the same all at the same time.

I took a deep breath and I walked away, I actually began to realize that I was late for work, I guess I spent about three hours talking to my kids. On my walk to work, each step I took felt as if my soul was shattering, piece by piece, centimeter by centimeter, inch by inch, heart beat by heartbeat. I heard my soul finally cry, I heard the sound as it left my body, something so cruel, something so scary, something so frightening as if hell had set me free. I stood at the gate of my employers, afraid to walk any further, hoping that they had no heard my eerie cries, of what sounded like a mad woman. I returned to a composed person, the fake façade, which I had grown accustomed to portraying for the pass 4 decades. I knew if I could make it to the stables near the cows, I would be ok.

As I approached the field, I heard a voice say you can rest now, I sat on the ground and I fell asleep, but actually I did not fall asleep, I died right there, never to return again. Sitis looked up me and smiled, but by this time, I wasn't worth a wet paper bag, I was on the floor of that airport holding the woman tightly crying and not caring who saw me, I had lost all thoughts of reason. It was as if I had lived her life and watched it from the inside of wife. She hugged me and said hush child it's alright. I looked down and found myself cradled to the floor as if I was an infant embryo, just being released from the womb.

I sat up, still on the floor, then I dried my eyes and as with any good reporter, I asked her, how she could pull that story together to make it so believable? she smiled and said Because I am Uzit, I am Sitidos, I am Sitis and I am the Woman they Call Wife. I was Her and She was Me. I then as a reporter became so confused, I said that cannot be true, how could you have died? the story says, Job was restored, and he was given 10 more children, the story said all he had was restored, to 100-folds. She smiled and said, that is true, all was restored to Job and his next wife, her name was Dinah, she was one of Jacobs daughters.

I guess if I was a jealous woman, I could now find myself very angry with Job and God, because, some would say, why did I suffer and when it was time to restore I died, and he was allowed to live in that phrase where, (Your latter shall be greater), But, I can say with certainty, that my husband's latter was great, because sometime after my death he eventually was restored, and was allowed to proceed in life. And I guess my greatest latter was to die and live in a quiet peace. Where I did not have to cry all day, mourn all day, suffer all day, and live in turmoil all night. I guess if I had been a truly angry woman, I would have found it difficult to be happy for my husband, and his new family, in his latter greatness.

But I am not, because I loved my husband, the father of my children, the king of my queen, the apple of my eye, my protector and my provider. Those were the reasons I never left, worked hard, attended to his needs, cooked, cleans and scrubbed floors for us, aided his health the best I could. Those were the reasons I left my pain inside of me, smiled when I wanted to cry, held my head high when I wish I could die, Because I respected my husband, I respected God, I just did not understand, why I had to lose so much, I guess that was the part that says through sickness and health or that we leave and cleave.

I do not presume to understand gods plans, because he said; "his plans were not like ours" and that I would not know when he was coming or going and if this is true then it is true.

I then heard the screeching of a car horn, I woke up out of a deep sleep, sitting straight up in my bed, I thought, I just interviewed Wife. I then rolled out of bed, sat at my computer and I composed her words, it was so amazing, I felt so honored to be chosen to bring that Lady's truth to life. I did not understand much, but in my heart, I was saying thank you Lord for choosing me, God and Her (Wife) needed me to tell her story, (And I needed a second chance to redeem my story as a Journalist, I needed a second chance to bring some luster back into my nonexistent, frozen, dismantled life) she needs the world to hear her side of the events, she needed for the true accounts of her life to be recognized. She did not ask me to change it, she did not deny her part, she did not deny her words, she did not deny her anguish, pain, grief, hatred or malice. She did not lay the blame on anyone else, she just needed it all told and understood, she needed people to examine their lives and see if they would or could truly say, they would have done it differently, so here it is.

God is always in Control, but he doesn't always take control, sometimes he just let it happen.

Acknowledgement of Usage:

Scriptures used from the KJV

Butterfly and Bee Consulting,

Marketing and Media Group (2023)

Poem from: My Inside Voices,

"Rebirthing Ourselves"

Author: Rose Griffin (2020)

Rebirthing Ourselves

When we remove bitterness from our lives and hearts, what we're actually doing is reactivating the sweet juices of love, hope, success and peace that resides inside of us.

Bitterness is like drinking something without flavor, for a while it doesn't work well with your taste buds, but after an extended period of time, you find yourself growing accustomed to that taste.

Without realizing it, you have conformed your whole world to that action. Without thinking about it, we spend years and decades thinking bitterness is the taste for us, we find absolutely nothing wrong with that course of lifestyle.

In fact we find ways and means of making sure, we have adequate excuses for that very same style. Even to the point, that we become perfect at convincing ourselves and others, we are supposed to do it in that manner.

If we use tea for an example, once upon a time, sweet, lemony, mango, tangerine or some other added flavor is how we enjoyed it. And through a course if incidences, doctors' advice, lifestyle tips, recommendation, pains, inability to trust, heart wrenching situations and failures, we end our relationships without flavor or sweetness.

Vowing never to return again. For most of us being stubborn and set in our ways, we stick to said actions and advice, being it warranted, intentional or forced upon us. We stand strong and firm in our decisions and beliefs.

Even on those days where we accidentally find ourselves glaring at a glass across the room, which has a frozen chill illuminated from it, with peach slivers and visions of ice streaming down the side of the glass.(our desires)

Deep inside of our "made up minds"!!! we at that very moment, knows for sure we desire that glass and all its contents. But we take a deep breath and look away. That glass represent change, new, freshness, happy, laughter, soul searching and a return to our lives.

But because that still voice says "no, don't, you'd better not, remember the last time". We close our eyes, desire and hands, to what our hearts says yes too. In those moments without physically knowing it, a piece of our free selves disappears, leaving us bitter inside.

Bitter because each time we say no to happiness, desire, achievements or just plain life, we disappear from ourselves, leaving a void. That void turns cold because our souls long for freedom to be at peace with our earthly eyesight and instincts.

Only to wake up one day, sadden and emotionally bankrupted. We as warm blooded, achieving, intelligent, loving, protecting, renounced, spectacular human being. We are more than "less than", we are endowed from birth with so many gifts and bitterness wasn't one, we grow that gift like cabbage in a field of our minds and allow it to take control of our lives.

The saddest part of all is, most of us are so settled in this course, we aren't aware this is where we are, how we live, what we do. We have totally emerged our lives in this function, until we have actually forgotten how real life, love, energy, peace, laughter and soul satisfying feels or looks. Our tea(souls) screams for clean oxygen, pure flavor, and chance to live again

I was lying in bed, thinking on ways to improve the best of me and I began to write.
(c) 2020 Rose Griffin.

Dear Readers,

I am Rose Griffin the Author of My Inside Voices the Series, Along with Ready for the Wedding, Not prepared for the Marriage. The Politician and I, and Also: Interviewing The Woman Called Wife.

I am a Mother, Grandmother, Godmother, Daughter and Eldest Sister, (all of these titles I cherish the most). But along with these personal titles, I stand in gratitude for my Degree in Psychology, My Certifications as an Addictions Specialist, My Certifications and Ordinations as Evangelist, My Jobs as Director of two 501c3, Non-Profit Organizations: Bent Isn't Broken and Understand Inc, Advocacy Group. I feel grateful every day for the opportunity to practice my gifts.

Made in the USA
Columbia, SC
22 August 2023

21884618R00072